THE TURN
OF THE SCREW

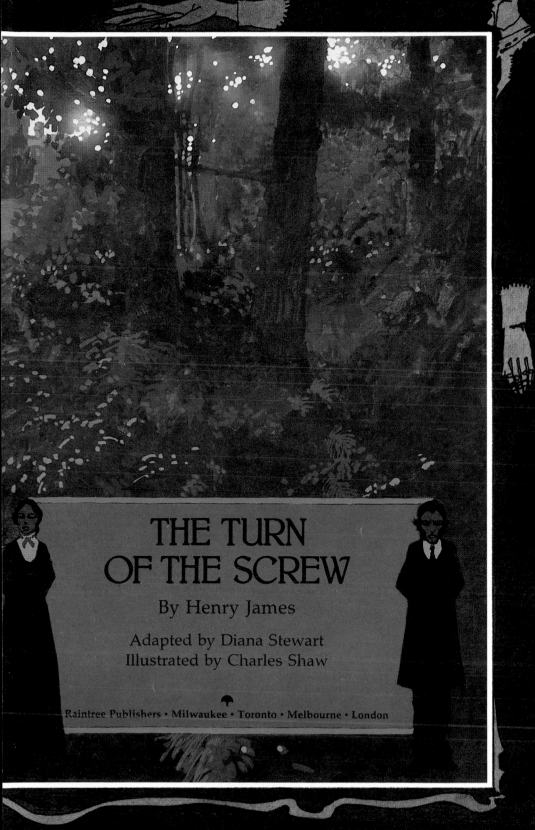

THE TURN
OF THE SCREW

By Henry James

Adapted by Diana Stewart
Illustrated by Charles Shaw

Raintree Publishers • Milwaukee • Toronto • Melbourne • London

Library of Congress Number: 81-5217

4 5 6 7 8   89 88 87 86 85

Printed in the United States of America.

Library of Congress Cataloging in Publication Data

Stewart, Diana.
    The turn of the screw.

    (Raintree short classics)
    Summary: The governess of two enigmatic children
fears their souls are in danger from the ghosts of
previous governess and her sinister lover.
    1. I. Shaw, Charles, 1941-   II. James, Henry,
1843-1916. Turn of the screw. III. Title. IV. Series.
PZ7.S84878Tu   [Fic.]   81-5217
ISBN 0-8172-1672-3   lib. bdg.
ISBN 0-8172-2027-5 softcover

CONTENTS

CHAPTER I

I was twenty years old when I left my father's home (a vicarage in central England) to answer an advertisement in a London newspaper. The position listed was that of a governess. The man who advertised was like no one I had ever met before in my simple life. He was young, handsome, pleasant, and kind. Money was no worry for him, and I suspected that his time was spent in using his wealth entirely for his own pleasure and entertainment.

His London house was large and filled with expensive items he had picked up in his travels around the world. The position he advertised, however, was not there. He wanted me to travel to Essex — to his country estate.

Two years before, he had been left guardian to a small nephew and niece, children of a brother and his wife who had been killed in India. The care of these two young charges worried him greatly. He was a bachelor, and he had no interest in tying himself down with a home and family.

Since he had no other relations to look after the children, he had sent them to the country and hired the best people he could find to look after them. An older woman — Mrs. Grose — was in charge of the house and the servants. For a while he had employed another young woman as governess, but she had gone. The boy Miles had then been sent to a boarding school, but he would be home soon for his summer holidays.

For two days, I considered whether or not to accept the

position. The life, I knew, would be lonely, but the salary he offered me was more than I could have ever expected. And then, too, I knew that in my heart I wanted to do anything I could to please this man.

When I went to see him a second time, I agreed to take the job. I could see the pleasure and relief on his face, and my heart was filled with joy. He had only one condition that I must obey, he said. He wanted me to take very good care of my little charges, but I was to never — never! — bother him with the details of their lives or education. He wanted no letters, no reports, no questions asked. He only wanted to continue to live his carefree life.

In my heart I vowed never to worry my wonderful, handsome employer. He would be delighted with the way I did my job!

The June day was still bright and beautiful when I arrived in the village of Bly — the town nearest my employer's country estate. I remember very well my first sight of my new home. The house itself was very old but well kept. It was surrounded by woods, lawns, gardens, and fields. There was even a small lake a short distance from the house. I found it difficult to understand why my employer spent so little time in such a lovely setting.

A carriage had been waiting for me in Bly, and as we approached the house, I saw two maids peeking out from the downstairs windows. Mrs. Grose, the housekeeper, was waiting to greet me at the front door. With her was the little girl Flora. I knew the moment I met the kindly older woman that we would become friends.

Flora was eight and a beautiful little angel. I was sure it would be a joy to teach and love such a wonderful child. Her brother Miles was due to return home in two days time.

"Is Miles as lovely as his sister?" I asked Mrs. Grose as we sat together later over a cup of tea.

"Oh, miss!" she replied. "If you think Flora is wonderful, wait until you see the little gentleman!"

I was indeed looking forward to meeting Miles. We had received a note saying he would arrive on the public coach on Friday morning. Flora and I made plans to go into Bly to meet him. I knew from the happiness on her face that her brother was very dear to her.

Thursday morning — much to my surprise and pleasure — I received a letter from my employer. I immediately recognized his strong, bold writing on the envelope. Inside was just a brief note along with another envelope. This second letter was unopened.

"This letter," wrote my employer, "is from the headmaster at Miles's school. He is an awful bore. Read it, please. Deal with him. But please don't report to me. Not a word! I am off on my travels!"

I broke the seal on the headmaster's letter and read it. I could hardly believe my eyes! The child Miles had been dismissed from school. He would never be permitted to go back again. I read the astonishing letter over twice and then sought out the housekeeper.

"Please, Mrs. Grose," I said. "Can you tell me what you think of this? Miles has been dismissed from school!"

"Dismissed!" the good woman cried. "But why? What has he done?" As she raised her face to mine, I saw that her eyes were filled with tears. "There must be some terrible mistake."

"I don't understand it myself," I said slowly. "The letter does not give any details. The headmaster simply states that they will not keep him there any longer. He says that Miles is a problem to the other students — that the boy is a bad influence on his classmates."

"Master Miles a problem? Bad? Never!" she declared firmly. "Why, the sweet boy is only ten years old! While he was here, he never gave me a minute's worry. Why, sometimes I wished that he had a little more spirit even. Young boys should get into mischief now and then, you know. It's only natural."

"This does seem very strange," I replied.

"You wait, miss! You wait until you see Miles. Then see what you think!"

I was now very impatient to meet my young charge. Another question, however, had been bothering me.

"Tell me, Mrs. Grose," I said. "I understand that the children had another governess last year. What was she like?"

"Miss Jessel? She was also young and pretty — almost as young and as pretty as you, miss," Mrs. Grose said carefully.

"Did the children like her?"

"Oh, yes, miss. They liked her very much. 'Specially Miss Flora."

Without knowing why, I felt that Mrs. Grose was keeping something from me. "But she left?" I asked, curious.

"Well, miss, she died," was the housekeeper's startling reply.

"Died! Here in the house?"

"No, she went off," Mrs. Grose continued slowly. "She left to go home at the end of the year for a holiday. But she never came back, and I heard from the master that she was dead. Master Miles was sent away to school, and the housemaids and I looked after Miss Flora. That was about six months ago."

She returned to her work, and I was left to my own thoughts. The whole situation seemed strange to me. Why was nothing more said about the other governess than that she had died? She had been a young woman. Certainly that was odd.

I tried to put off my worries as Flora and I set out the next day to meet young Master Miles. Our carriage was a little late arriving, and he stood waiting for us in the door of the inn. I saw at once that everything Mrs. Grose said about him was true. Miles was a perfectly beautiful child. As he took my hand, he seemed filled with love and tenderness. There was such a look of goodness and purity about him. I found it impossible to believe that this boy could possibly

be a bad influence on anyone. Surely the headmaster was mistaken!

I wasn't sure just what I ought to do about the matter of his school. In normal circumstances, I would have written his uncle, but my employer had asked me to deal with the headmaster's letter, and I wanted badly to please him. The whole summer holidays were ahead of us. I would wait a while and say nothing. There was plenty of time.

During the days that followed, I came to love the two charges in my care. We played and studied and laughed together. They were both very bright, intelligent children. No teacher could have asked for better, more hard-working students. My first impression — that they were sweet, lovely angels — did not change. They obeyed me instantly. I never had to scold or correct them. Their manners were excellent. In fact, I had never known such well-behaved, polite children.

The summer days were long, and each evening when Flora and Miles were in bed, it became a habit with me to take a walk around the grounds. The estate was very large and beautiful, and I found great pleasure in strolling through the fields and along the garden paths.

One evening as I took my walk, I thought about my employer. I was so happy here. Only one thing could have made me happier. I wished that the man in London — the children's uncle — could see how well I was doing. I was proud of my work, and I wanted him to be proud of me. For a moment I allowed myself to dream. In my dream I turned on the path and he was there, smiling at me.

Slowly I walked back towards the house. Suddenly I had a shock. For a moment I thought that my dream had come true!

The house was built with two towers — one on either end. At the top of the tower on the right stood a man, and I could feel his eyes on me. As I looked more closely, however, I saw that the figure was not that of my employer. This was not the man I had seen in London. In fact, this was not a man I had ever seen before!

CHAPTER II

As I continued to stare, I felt a deathly hush settle over my little world. Not a whisper of wind stirred the trees, and the birds overhead stopped their singing.

The figure on the tower turned to face me, and his eyes burned into my soul. For a long time we stared at one another. He was too far away to call to. He stood very tall. Both of his hands were on the stone ledge around the tower. A minute passed, and he moved. Slowly he walked across the platform. His hand trailed along the rough stone ledge. I had the firm impression that even as he walked, his eyes never left my face. Finally, he stopped at one corner of the tower, and then he turned away and was gone.

In my mind I tried to find a dozen answers for who he might be. Perhaps he was a visitor from the village. Perhaps he was a new servant. But I knew everyone in the village nearby, and Mrs. Grose would have told me if a new man had been hired. Finally, I had to conclude that the man was a trespasser who had somehow managed to get into the house and up to the tower.

The evening was warm, but a shiver shook me. Why had the man frightened me so? He was only one man, and the house was filled with servants. Surely I had nothing to fear.

I can't say how long I stayed on the path, staring at the tower. I only remember that when I returned to the house, night had fallen. Mrs. Grose met me anxiously at the door.

I had never stayed out so long, and the good woman was worried.

To this day, it seems strange to me that I did not tell her about the man I had seen. Perhaps I was ashamed of my fears and didn't want to worry her about nothing. So I said nothing. I simply made an excuse about having walked farther than I had realized.

My work in the house continued as usual. Miles and Flora were a constant joy to me. Both the children had a gentleness about them. And as I came to know Miles better, I found the letter from his headmaster more and more absurd. He was so kind and loving and he called me his dear.

The only thing that did surprise me was that he never mentioned school at all. He never talked about his friends there or his teachers. In fact, he never spoke at all about his past. It was as though his life had begun when I first met him at the inn.

One Sunday it was raining too hard for us to attend morning services at the village church. I decided that if the weather improved, we would go to the evening meeting.

By afternoon the rain had stopped, and we got ready for the walk into the village. Just before we left, however, I remembered that I had put my gloves in the dining room earlier.

The sky was still gray, but there was enough light to allow me to see. My gloves were lying on a chair near the window. As I crossed the room, I was aware of a person on the outside looking straight in. It was the same man I had seen on the tower a few days before!

I caught my breath in shock and felt a sudden coldness over my entire body. It was the same man, but this time he was much nearer than before. The window of the dining room was on the ground floor, and I could see him clearly from the waist up. His face was close to the glass. He remained only for a few seconds, but it was long enough to convince me that he had recognized me — just as I had

recognized him. He stared into my face hard and deep, and I can still see those strange eyes in my memory. But even as he stared, I knew without a doubt that he had not come in search of me. He had come looking for someone else.

This thought gave me courage, and I ran out of the door, around the side of the house. I rushed to the window where he had stood — and found no one! I stopped and almost dropped to the ground in relief. The relief, however, did not last long. He was nowhere in sight, but I felt his presence as strongly as ever. He was there, but he was not there!

Instead of returning immediately to the house, I walked to the window. I pressed my face to the glass and looked in, just as the man had done.

Mrs. Grose was standing in the dining room. She saw me just as I had seen the strange visitor. She stopped short and stared, and I saw her face turn white. I knew that in a minute she would come around to find me. What would I tell her?

"What is the matter?" she gasped a few moments later. Her face was now flushed and she was out of breath. "You're white as a sheet. You look awful!"

I put out my hand to her and she took it. Just her touch made me feel better.

"Has anything happened?" she asked anxiously.

"Yes," I said. "You must know it has. Did I look very strange?"

"Through the window? Yes! Dreadful!"

"Well," I replied slowly, "what you saw in the dining room just now is what I saw — just before. Only I saw something much worse!"

Her hand tightened in mine. "What was it?"

"A strange man. Looking in."

"What man?" Her eyes grew wide and frightened.

"I haven't the least idea," I replied.

"Have you seen him before?"

"Yes — once. On the old tower."

"But you never said a word!" she gasped. "Was it a gentleman? Perhaps someone from the village?"

"No!" I said firmly. "It was no gentleman. He was horrible! He was . . . Heaven help me if I know *what* he was!"

"What did he look like?" Her hand trembled in mine as she asked.

"He had red hair, very red, and curly. His face was pale and long and thin. Some people might even think him handsome. He had queer whiskers that were as red as his hair. His eyebrows were darker. His eyes! They were strange and sharp — awful! And his mouth was wide with thin lips."

Mrs. Grose turned pale as I talked. "Quint!" she exclaimed at last.

"Quint?" I echoed.

"Peter Quint — the master's own servant, his valet. The Master left him here in charge when he went away."

"Well, what became of him?" I asked, puzzled.

Her expression became very frightened. "He went away, too."

"Went where?" I asked impatiently.

"God knows where! He died!"

"Died!" I almost shrieked.

"Yes. Mr. Quint is dead!"

CHAPTER III

In the days that followed, Mrs. Grose and I talked about Peter Quint at length.

"Did the children know Peter Quint?" I asked.

"Oh, very well indeed," Mrs. Grose sighed. "Miles particularly spent a great deal of time with him. He and Quint were great friends. I would have put a stop to it if I could, but it wasn't my place."

"You didn't like him?"

"No, miss, I didn't!" she said firmly. "Not a bit. He was bad through and through. And clever. Oh, so clever. But you never knew what he was thinking. It made my heart just about break to see Master Miles trailing after him. Quint spoiled the boy, he did. Took him with him everywhere —" She stopped as she saw the troubled look on my face. "What is it, my dear?" she asked. "What's the matter?"

I had indeed grown pale, for the most terrible idea had come to me. "I told you," I said slowly, "that Quint was not looking for me when I saw him in the dining room. His eyes went past me. They searched the room looking for someone else. Could that someone have been Miles?"

"I don't know, miss!" the older woman said anxiously.

"Tell me more about Quint!" I insisted.

A flush spread over her face. "I don't know if I can tell you, miss! Oh, the people in the village told such stories about him. They were too terrible to repeat. He was wicked — evil! That was why I hated to see Master Miles so fond of the man. I couldn't stand the thought of Quint leading the boy into his wicked ways. I tried to tell the master once, but he's so kind, he can't see bad in anyone."

"How did Quint die?" I asked.

"It was last winter. His body was found dead on the road from the village. The night was cold and icy. He had been drinking. Somehow, people believe, he took the wrong path home that night and slipped on the steep slope. His head was broken. Oh, miss! Do you really think he's come back from the grave to see Master Miles? What would the child do if he saw him? It would be terrible! Maybe we'd better write to the master — tell him what you saw."

"No, Mrs. Grose," I said quickly. "Do you really think he'd believe it if we told him a story about Peter Quint coming back from the dead?" I blushed at the idea of what my employer would say. He would probably believe that I was just using this as an excuse to see him again.

"So what will we do?" she asked anxiously.

"There is nothing we can do. We can only make very sure that the children are never left alone. They must be either with you or me!"

I cannot tell you how anxious I felt. I was responsible for these innocent children. We were cut off, really, from the rest of the world. They had no one to care about them but me.

From that moment on, I kept them very near to me. Flora slept in one end of my room. Miles was just next door. All went well for a time. Then, one afternoon I left Miles with Mrs. Grose and took Flora out to play by the lake.

Suddenly I was aware that someone was watching us from the other side of the water. The trees were thick on that side, but still I was sure that someone was there. At first I didn't think anything about it. It could have been a traveler or a neighbor.

Then the figure moved, and I saw it was a woman — no woman I had ever seen before. She was dressed entirely in

black, and her black hair was neatly pulled back into a bun. She was beautiful, with a strange, haunting beauty. But her face was pale. It looked white against her black hair and dress. It wasn't, however, anything I saw that made me shiver. Even from the distance, I felt her eyes first on me and then on Flora. As clearly as anything, I felt the presence of evil.

Quickly I looked at Flora. She was playing a little way from where I sat. I saw her glance at the woman and then look away. I *knew* she had seen the figure, but she didn't say a word. She continued to play with a flat piece of wood. Her whole attention seemed to be focused on the stick. Something was wrong — terribly wrong! Flora was *too* quiet, *too* uninterested. It was not natural. We had no visitors on the estate. A stranger must be noticed.

Suddenly Flora turned and met my eyes, and I read the truth there: This mysterious woman was no stranger to her. The child knew who she was, but still she said nothing. An odd light glowed in her eyes for a moment. Then, she smiled and the glow was gone.

Once back at the house, I went immediately to Mrs. Grose.

"I saw another person — a woman!" I said, trembling. "She was dressed in black." Quickly I described the figure I had seen. "Oh, Mrs. Grose," I cried. "I felt such a presence of evil!"

Mrs. Grose turned pale and dropped into a chair. "Miss Jessel!" she cried.

"Miss Jessel? The governess?" I felt all the color leaving my face.

"Yes!"

"Tell me about her," I said quietly. "I have to know."

"I don't know how to tell you, miss," Mrs. Grose said anxiously, dropping her eyes to her hands in her lap. "She . . . well, she was a lady, but she wasn't a good woman. She was young and beautiful, but she went around with that man."

"What man? Quint?" I questioned.

"Yes. Peter Quint! A wicked man he was, but the women all liked him. They ran after him, and he had his way with all the ladies here about."

"Miss Jessel, too?" I asked solemnly.

"Yes, Miss Jessel, too. They took to each other right away, and finally she had to leave. She paid for her sins. I — I don't know how she died. Miss Flora cried and cried when I told her Miss Jessel wouldn't be back."

Slowly some things were becoming clear to me. Miss Jessel was back. She had come to find Flora, just as Quint had come looking for Miles. Had these two lost souls already seen the children? Had they talked to them? Were my darlings already in great danger?

I waited and watched in the days that followed. Just for a minute by the lake I had seen a look in Flora's eyes that frightened me, and I studied both her and Miles very carefully. I don't even know when I was aware of a change in them. Oh, on the surface, they seemed perfectly normal. The change I felt came from within them.

As the days passed and nothing new happened, I began to wonder if I was only imagining that the children were somehow different. Still I kept noticing things about them. They never quarreled as I had seen so many brothers and sisters do. In fact, the closeness and understanding between them was very unusual. It was as though they shared some secret. Often Miles would put his arm around his sister and whisper in her ear. She would smile and nod. Yes, there was a strange bond between them.

And I was afraid I knew what it was — Quint and Miss Jessel!

Then one night I sat reading in my room. The light from my candle did not reach as far as the bed where Flora slept, but I could hear by her breathing that she was asleep.

As I was about to turn a page, something stopped me. I had the definite feeling that something was stirring outside my door. For a long moment I listened, but now I

could hear nothing. Finally, I took my candle and opened the door. Nothing was there. Carefully I locked the door behind me and moved to the door of Miles's room. All was quiet.

At this point, a sudden gust of air blew out my candle, but by the light of the moon, I saw that someone was on the stairs! For the third time, I saw Peter Quint!

The man had reached the landing halfway up. Suddenly he stopped short. He had caught sight of me. His eyes were fixed on me just as they had been from the tower and from the window. I felt the danger and evil in him, but strangely I felt no terror. I held my place. I would not let him get past me to Miles's room. I continued to stare at him in the terrible silence. At last when I thought I could not stand it any longer, he turned and went back down the staircase and into the darkness.

Now each night I waited until the children were asleep. Then, I took my candle and went out into the hall. I never saw Quint there again, but what I did see was just as frightening. Looking down from the top of the stairs one night, I saw a figure seated on the bottom steps — Miss Jessel! Her back was to me and her head was bowed. Her whole figure had the look of such terrible sadness. I only saw her for a minute, and then she was gone.

A few nights later as the clock struck one, I awoke from a sound sleep. I had left a candle burning, but now it was out. Quickly I struck a match. What I saw brought me out of bed. Flora's bed was empty! The door, however, was still locked. She had not left the room. I glanced at the window. The drapes were partly closed, but I could see that Flora was behind them, staring out the window into the night.

Quietly I left the room. I wanted to see what the child was looking at. Quickly I went down the stairs to the room below mine. Through the window I looked out onto the back lawn. The moon lighted up the night, and I could see a person standing motionless, staring up towards the house. Another figure stood on the tower above. The person on the lawn was not the one I expected to see. It was my own little Miles!

I rushed out of the house, and when I held out my hand to him, he took it.

"What are you doing?" I asked. "Tell me the truth! Why did you come out?"

"Did I frighten you?" he asked gaily. I can still see his wonderful smile. "Well, did I? You see, I wanted to do something *bad* for a change. I wanted to play a joke on you." And he bent forward and kissed me.

I didn't believe him for a moment. I was now convinced that he had come to see Peter Quint. I was sure as I could possibly be that the four of them — Quint, Miss Jessel, Flora, and Miles — were secretly meeting!

Now I was haunted by a new fear. The things I had seen and felt had been terrible, but had the children seen even *more* — things terrible, evil, and unknown?

Oh, I can't tell you the number of times I wanted to confront them. I wanted to shout and rage: "They're here! They're here, aren't they? You see them! Don't deny it! I know you see them and talk to them!"

But I didn't dare say a word. I had no idea what harm I might do.

Just when I thought I couldn't stand their silence any longer, they would be sweeter, more loving to me than ever. Was it possible that they were living such a lie? Was it possible that they were so evil already that they would lie and deceive me? Could I have lost them already?

CHAPTER IV

One Sunday morning in the beginning of the fall, we were walking to church. Mrs. Grose and Flora had gone on ahead. I was suddenly aware that there was a new change in Miles. As I write down his words, I realize that they said little. It is what Miles left *unsaid* that frightened me. His voice was still sweet and childish as he stopped me near the door of the church.

"Fall is here, my dear," he said. "When am I going back to school?"

His question took me by surprise. He had never mentioned school, and I had decided that he would be safest at home with me where I could watch him.

"Were you happy at school?" I asked lightly.

"Oh, I'm happy anywhere. It is just that I want to see — well, more of life. I want my own kind."

"And Flora isn't your own kind?" I asked carefully.

"She's only a baby girl. But I love her." He frowned. "And you too. If I didn't —"

"Yes," I prompted. "If you didn't?" I looked at the graves in the churchyard while I waited for him to answer.

"Well, you know what!" He paused for a moment. "Does my uncle think what *you* think?"

"And what do I think?" I asked. I sat down on a stone before my legs collapsed under me. Was I going to hear the truth from him at last?

"I don't know for certain," was all he replied. "You don't tell. But I mean, does *he* know?"

"Know what?" I insisted.

"Why, the way I'm going on, of course."

"I — I don't think he really cares," I said. I knew I was not being very loyal to my employer, but I didn't know what else to say.

"Then make him care," Miles said softly.

"What do you mean?" The look on his face was suddenly making me very nervous.

"I think he should come down here. If you won't write to him, I will!" He smiled at me brightly, but his eyes were filled with a gleam that made me tremble.

Miles knew! He knew how I felt about his uncle! Now he was using this knowledge — the fear I had of writing him — to get what he wanted. And what he wanted was the freedom to come and go as he liked. He wanted to be free to meet and talk with Quint without my interference.

Suddenly I felt sick and frightened. For the first time since I had known Miles, I wanted to get away from him. Quietly I sent him on into the church, but I couldn't force myself to follow. I couldn't stand the thought of sitting beside him.

More than that, I couldn't stand the thought of staying in Bly, of seeing either Miles or Flora ever again. I had taken such pride in my work. I had wanted to please my employer so badly. I wanted him to remember me and think well of me. If Miles wrote to him, what would he think? He would think that I was tired of being alone in the country. He would believe that I wanted him to come to me!

Oh, I could see the amusement on his face! He was so rich and handsome. He must have many women chasing after him, trying to get his attention. I could not stand the thought that he would think that of me, also.

I wouldn't stay! I would leave. I would turn my back on the evil that haunted the house. Now would be the perfect time. Mrs. Grose and the children wouldn't be back for some time.

I hurried home. Once inside, I sank onto the steps to rest a moment. Then I realized that it was on this very spot — not a month before — that I had seen Miss Jessel in the darkness of the night. I ran up to the schoolroom to gather my things, but as I opened the door, a horrible sight met my eyes.

Seated at my table was the woman herself! She rose as I entered. She looked terrible in her black dress. Her face was pale with misery and sadness. We were no more than a dozen feet apart when our eyes met. She seemed to say to me that she had every right to sit at that table. It had been her table before it was mine.

"You terrible, miserable woman!" I cried, and my voice rang down the long hallway and through the empty house. She looked at me as though she had heard and understood me. And then there was nothing in the room but sunlight. I knew, then, that I could not leave. I had to stay and fight these terrible, evil forces. I had to try and save Miles and Flora!

By the time Mrs. Grose and the children returned from church, I had reached a decision. I could not allow Miles to believe I was weak. I could not put myself in his power.

"Mrs. Grose," I said when I found the housekeeper in the kitchen. "I saw *her* again."

"Where?" And the good woman trembled.

"In the schoolroom. She is suffering. She suffers the tortures of the lost — or the damned. Whatever it is, she wants Flora, and I don't know what more I can do to save her. I think the time has come to send for their uncle."

"Oh, yes, miss. Do!"

"I don't know what I can tell him when he arrives. I don't know what I can say. But at least I can show him the letter from the headmaster."

That night I wrote the dreaded letter to my employer and laid it on the table in the hall for one of the servants to mail. Before I went to sleep, I took a candle to look in on Miles. He was still awake.

"You're not asleep?" I asked as I sat beside him on the bed.

"No. I was lying here thinking," he replied.

"And what do you think of?"

"I think you know about this queer business of ours."

He took my hand. His was cool and firm in mine. I held my breath for a minute and then asked: "What queer business, Miles?"

"Oh, you know, you know!"

"Miles," I said quietly, "I've written your uncle." He was silent, and I couldn't tell what he was thinking. "Do you know, Miles," I continued, "you've never told me about your school. You never mention your friends or teachers. You know that the school won't let you go back, don't you. Never."

"I don't want to go back," he said firmly. "I want to go to a new place. Oh, you know what a boy wants."

"Oh, Miles!" I cried. "I want you to tell me what happened — before you came back and before you went away!"

"Nothing happened!" But I caught the slight quivering in his voice. It made me drop to my knees beside him and clutch his hand harder in mine.

"Oh, Miles! Dear little Miles! If you only knew how much I want to help you! I'd rather die than give you pain. I'd rather die than hurt a hair of your head. I just want you to help me to save you!"

For a moment I thought I had won. His eyes were on mine, and I saw his lips open to speak. Then suddenly there came a cold blast of air through the room. The room shook as though a great wind was rushing through the window. The boy gave a loud, high shriek. I couldn't tell if it was a scream of joy or terror. I jumped to my feet. The candle had blown out, but in the light of the moon, I saw that the window was tightly closed and the drapes were still — but the room was cold from the wind.

CHAPTER V

The next day Miles was more charming and loving than ever. Our talk of the night before seemed to be forgotten. After lunch he took me by the hand. "Come," he said, leading me to the music room. "Come and let me play for you."

I couldn't resist his pleading eyes or the appeal in his voice. He sat down at the old piano and played as I had never heard him play before. On and on he played, and I was delighted. The music was so lovely that I lost track of time. Suddenly I realized I had no idea what Flora was doing!

"Where's Flora?" I asked Miles.

"My dear," he said, still playing, "how should I know?"

I went straight to the schoolroom, but she wasn't there. Next, I looked for Mrs. Grose. The good woman hadn't seen her. She was as worried as I was. Together we searched the house. There was no sign of the little girl. All at once, I knew where to find her.

"Come with me!" I called to Mrs. Grose. "I know where she is! She's with *her*! We must find them!"

"But where is Master Miles?" she asked anxiously.

"He tricked me. He kept me busy so Flora could get away. By now he's probably with Quint."

We went quickly to the lake where I had seen Miss Jessel for the first time. There was no one in sight. Mrs. Grose looked at me anxiously. "She's not here!" she cried.

"Wait! The boat is gone! She's taken it to the other side."

"All alone — that child?" she gasped.

"She's not alone, and at such times she's not a child. She's an old, old woman. Come, we have to walk around the lake. It will only take us a few minutes."

I hurried as fast as I could, but often I had to slow down to give the housekeeper time to catch her breath. At last we arrived on the far side of the lake. It was just as I had thought. The boat had been pulled up on shore and hidden in the bushes. The heavy oars had been placed inside.

"There she is!" we both exclaimed at once.

Flora stood before us on the grass, smiling. She did not move as we hurried forward. Mrs. Grose ran to her and hugged her close. The child didn't say a word, and I'd be hanged if I'd speak first. She looked smugly at me, still smiling.

"Where's Miles?" she asked at last.

"I'll tell you, my pet," I said softly, "if you'll tell me where Miss Jessel is."

Suddenly the whole affair was out in the open. I saw the quick burning look in her eyes. The strange gleam nearly took my breath away. The stillness was abruptly shattered by a shriek. It could have been a wounded or frightened animal — but I knew it wasn't. I turned and looked across the lake.

"She's there! She's there!" I cried, grabbing Mrs. Grose by the arm. Miss Jessel stood before us on the opposite side of the lake. Flora didn't blink but stared straight ahead. Mrs. Grose turned and gazed. A frown gathered on her wrinkled brow. "I don't see anything, miss!" she cried.

"She's there!" I repeated. "You see her, don't you, Flora!"

In an instant it seemed to me that all Flora's young beauty disappeared. I had said that she was old, and suddenly she looked to me hideous, hard, and ugly.

"I don't know what you mean!" she snarled. "I see nobody. I see nothing. I never have. I think you're mean. I don't like you!" And she turned and buried her head

in Mrs. Grose's skirt. "Take me away, take me away — from her!"

"From me?" I panted.

"From you — from you!" the girl cried.

I looked again at the figure across the lake. The wretched child had spoken as she had never spoken before. She spoke the words that had been told her by her evil friend. She was possessed. I had lost her!

"Go!" I cried to the housekeeper. "Take her away!"

I have no memory of what happened next. I knew that I must have fallen to the ground and lain there for a long time. When I raised my head again, it was dark.

Once back at the house I went directly to my room. I saw that all Flora's things had been removed. She was to spend the night with Mrs. Grose. I was so cold. I felt as though I could never be warm again. I had no idea where Miles was. He had his freedom now. I was almost stunned, therefore, when he suddenly appeared at my side. He looked at me, but he didn't say a word. Slowly he moved and sank down into a chair. We sat there in silence. Yet he wanted, I knew, to be with me.

Next morning I awoke to find Mrs. Grose beside me. "Flora is in a high fever this morning," she said. "Every three minutes she asks me if you are coming. She never wants to speak to you again she says."

"I know," I replied calmly. "She wants to get rid of me. But I won't go. Instead, she shall go."

"What do you mean, miss?" she asked startled.

"I want you to take Flora to her uncle. Take her away from *them*."

"You're right," Mrs. Grose cried. "I can't stay here either."

"Do you mean that since yesterday you've seen —?" I began.

"No," she said quickly. "I haven't *seen*, I've *heard*!"

"Heard what?"

"From the child — horrors! On my honor, miss, she says

such things — such terrible filth!" The housekeeper broke down and began to cry. "Shocking! The things she says are wicked — shocking! I've never heard anything like it. Where could she have learned such words!"

"I believe you know," I said solemnly. "The only answer is to get her away from them. There may be hope for her yet."

"There is one other thing," she said more quietly. "Your letter. It was never mailed."

"What became of it?"

"Goodness knows. Master Miles —"

"Do you mean that he took it?" I gasped.

"I don't know who else would have done. Do you think that's what happened at school? Do you think he stole?"

"I don't know. But don't worry about that now. I am going to find out. Mrs. Grose, Miles came to me last night. I believe he wanted to talk to me. The night before he was going to tell me about Quint — but he was stopped! Go to London, and leave him here with me. If only he will tell me about the evil — confess what he has seen and done — perhaps he can be saved."

CHAPTER VI

That night Miles and I had dinner together in the downstairs dining room. Here I felt again how my calmness depended on the success of my rigid will. I had to shut my eyes as tight as possible to the truth that what I had to deal with was, revoltingly, against nature. I had to get on by treating my monstrous ordeal as a push in an unpleasant direction, but demanding, after all, only another turn of the screw of ordinary human virtue.

Miles stood for a few minutes with his hands in his pockets, and looked as though he were about to speak. But all he said was: "I say, my dear, is she really very awfully ill?"

"Flora? She'll be better soon. London will make her feel better."

"Did the country disagree with her so suddenly?"

"No, I suppose we saw it coming on."

"Then why didn't you get her off before?"

"Before what?"

"Before she became too ill to travel."

I answered promptly. "She's *not* too ill to travel: she only might have been if she had stayed."

"I see, I see," said Miles.

Our meal was brief. When the maid had left the room, he turned to me. "Well — so we're alone!"

"Oh, more or less." I fancy my smile was pale. "Not absolutely. We shouldn't like that!" I went on.

"No. Of course we have the others. Do you mind being here with me?" he asked.

40

"Why should I mind?" I asked casually. "The only reason I stayed on was to be with you."

"You stayed on just for that?" he asked in surprise.

"Certainly. I am your friend. That shouldn't surprise you." My voice trembled a little. "Don't you remember what I told you that night in your room? I said that there was nothing in the world I wouldn't do for you."

"Oh, yes," he replied. I could tell that he was getting nervous. "You wanted me to tell you something."

"That's it. I wanted you to tell me what you have on your mind."

I knew he was becoming more and more upset. "Do you mean you want me to tell you now?" he asked.

"There couldn't be a better place or time."

He looked around uneasily, and for the first time I felt a new emotion in him — fear. It was as if he was suddenly afraid of me. But perhaps that was good.

"You want to go outside again, don't you," I said softly.

"Yes!" He tried to smile at me, but he seemed to be in pain. My heart ached for him. "Later I'll tell you everything," he added. "I'll tell you anything you like. I *will* tell you, but not now."

"Why not now?" I asked.

"I have to see one of the servants."

It was a lie, of course. "Very well," I replied calmly. "But before you go, just tell me one little thing. Tell me why you took my letter from the hall table yesterday."

Before he could make any reply, my attention was drawn to the window. There in full view stood Peter Quint. His white face of damnation was pressed against the glass. It was all I could do not to cry out. But I knew I could not! I had to keep Miles from seeing that horrible face. I was fighting that devil outside for a human soul — Miles's.

Miles had his back to the window, looking at me. I saw now that his face was covered with sweat and was as white as the evil devil outside. His hands reached out to me.

"Yes," he said. "I took the letter!"

I gave a cry of joy and hugged him close. I could feel the fever in his little body. His heart was pounding. I raised my eyes to the window and saw the thing move. It was like an angry, prowling beast. I knew I had Miles now, and I was going to keep him!

"Why did you take it?" I insisted.

"You were writing to my uncle. I wanted to see what you said about me. But you didn't say anything. You just asked him to come."

"Miles," I cried, "what did you do at school? Why won't they let you back?"

The look of pain returned to his face. "Well, I said things."

"Only that?"

"They thought it was enough."

"What were the things you said?"

He began to speak and then stopped. I looked again at the window. That white face of damnation was there, stopping his confession. Was I going to lose the fight? I pressed Miles against me and cried out: "No more, no more, no more!"

"Is *she* here?" Miles panted when he saw where I was looking.

"She?" I echoed.

"Miss Jessel, Miss Jessel!" he cried in fury.

At last he was admitting what he could see. "It's not Miss Jessel! But it's at the window — straight in front of us. It's there — that devil! But it's there for the last time!"

At this, his head began to shake. He flung himself at me in a terrible rage. The air seemed to be filled with the taste of poison — the very presence of evil.

"It's he?" Miles cried.

I was determined to have the whole truth out between us. "Whom do you mean by 'he'?"

"Peter Quint — you devil!" His eyes searched the room wildly. "Where!"

His words rang in my ears. He had confessed. He was mine now! I had won!

"What does it matter, my darling boy? What will he ever matter? *I* have you, and he has lost you forever!" I quickly turned him around to face the window. "There! Look!" I cried to Miles.

His eyes searched, but there was nothing to see but the quiet day. The terrible face of Peter Quint had gone. But even as I saw this, Miles let out a horrible cry. It had the ring of a creature in pain being thrown into darkness. I reached out and caught him as he began to fall. I caught him and I held him. It took me a minute to realize what I held. We were alone, all alone, and his little heart — free of the evil — had stopped.

Miles was dead.

GLOSSARY

advertisement (ad vər tīz′ mənt) a notice to the
 public, such as a notice printed in a newspaper

estate (is tāt′) the things a person owns; especially
 land and houses

governess (gəv′ ər nəs) a woman who takes care of
 and teaches a child in a private home

headmaster (hed′ mas tər) a man who is in charge of
 a private school

housekeeper (hau′ skē pər) a woman who is hired to
 keep a house in order

ordeal (or dēl′) a hard and painful experience

valet (val′ ət) a man's personal male servant